PROMISES

My Sister's Perfect Husband
by Rosemary Hayes
Illustrated by Giuliano Aloisi
Published by Ransom Publishing Ltd.
Unit 7, Brocklands Farm, West Meon, Hampshire GU32 1JN, UK
www.ransom.co.uk

ISBN   978 178591 257 3
First published in 2016

MY SISTER'S
PERFECT
HUSBAND

Rosemary Hayes

My name is Laila.

My mum says I have a lovely smile –
but she's just being kind.

I am definitely NOT beautiful. Not like my older sister.

My sister Mina is stunning. Everyone says so. She is tall and slim, with perfect skin and big dark eyes.

Mum and Dad are looking for a husband for Mina.

For months they have been introducing her to nice Pashtun boys.

The boys and their families come to our house. We sit around drinking tea and eating sweet stuff, and everyone talks to each other in a friendly way.

Everyone except Mina.

She's grumpy. She never smiles at the boys.

But they STILL want to marry her!

She's had lots of offers.

But Mina just shakes her head. She always finds fault.

Last night I heard my mum and dad talking.

'This is so embarrassing,' they said. 'We'll never find Mina a husband. At this rate, Laila will be married before Mina.'

That really scared me. I'm sixteen and I don't want to get married for a long time.

Actually, I'm not sure I EVER want to get married. But I can't say that to Mum and Dad.

I told my best friend, Serina, about
Mina.

'Well,' said Serina. 'You know what
we have to do?'

'What's that?' I asked.

Serina put her arm through mine. 'We'll have to find her a husband!'

'What?!' I said. 'How can we?'

'Leave it with me,' she said. 'I have an idea.'

'What do you mean?'

She put her finger to her lips. 'No more questions, Laila. Wait until tomorrow.'

The next day in class, Serina said,

'I know just the boy for Mina.'

'No way!' I said. 'Who is he?'

Then the teacher told us to stop
talking, so Serina whispered, 'I'll tell
you later.'

At break, she showed me some photos on her phone. Photos of a big family party.

'See this boy here?' she said, making the image bigger.

I stared at the face of a very
handsome young man.

'Wow! He's gorgeous! Who is he?'

'He's one of my cousins and he's called Karmal.'

I took another look at the photo, then I sighed.

'But how will he meet Mina? If Mum and Dad don't know him, they'll never invite him to the house.'

'I thought you said they were desperate to get Mina married?'

'Well … yes, but not *that* desperate.'

Serina frowned.

'Then we'll just have to make sure that Mina and Karmal meet up by accident.'

I stared at Serina. 'That won't work. My family's very strict. Mina would never be allowed to meet up with a boy on her own.'

'I said *by accident*,' said Serina. 'Now listen. Karmal is doing part-time work in the supermarket on Saturday mornings.'

'So?'

'Oh Laila, you are so stupid! Get your mum to take you and Mina shopping with her. Your mum goes to the supermarket every Saturday, right?'

'Well, yes … but … '

'Come on! You can find a way to get Mina there on Saturday. I'll go with my mum, too. Then we'll see Karmal at the supermarket and I can introduce him to Mina.'

I frowned. 'What if Mina doesn't fancy him?'

Serina laughed and held the picture of Karmal up to my face. You're kidding! How could anyone *not* fancy him?!'

I looked again.

He was very fit.

'Umm,' I said. 'But Mina's so fussy.'
Serina just raised her eyes to the sky. 'Be there on Saturday,' she said.

It wasn't going to be easy.

That night, at home, I said, 'Mina, will you come to the supermarket on Saturday with me and Mum?'

Mina was sitting in her bedroom, looking in the mirror. She was brushing her long, shiny black hair.

'Whatever for?' she asked.

I began to feel nervous. This wasn't going well.

'I need your advice,' I said.

Mina didn't turn round, but I could see her face in the mirror. She was frowning.

'Advice?' she said. 'What about?'

I didn't know what to say. Then suddenly I had an idea. I would pretend that I fancied Karmal and wanted to get to know him.

'It's about a boy,' I said.

I could feel myself blushing.

Mina put down her hairbrush and turned round. She stared at me and then she smiled.

'A boy, Laila!'

I nodded.

'Don't tell me you're in love?' she said.

I was feeling really uncomfortable now.

'Er … well … I don't know,' I stuttered.

'You can tell me about him, Laila. I promise I won't say anything to Mum and Dad.'

I didn't like lying to Mina, but I had to.

'His name's Karmal,' I said, my words all coming out in a rush. 'He's really nice. He's Serina's cousin and he works in the supermarket on Saturday mornings.'

'Hey, you're a sly one, Laila. So you want to go and see him at the supermarket?'

I nodded, feeling more and more embarrassed.

'How did you meet him?' she asked.

I had to tell her more lies.

'At Serina's house last week,' I said. 'He came in when Serina and I were doing homework together.'

'Umm,' said Mina, looking at her beautifully shaped fingernails. 'So why do you want me along? Surely you can manage without me?'

'Oh please, Mina. Please come with me. You know how shy I am with boys.'

Mina laughed. 'Oh, all right,' she said at last. 'I'll come. I'd like to see this guy you fancy so much.'

She got up and stretched, then she walked towards me and gave me a hug.

I looked up at her. I knew that Karmal would fall for her. All the boys did. And then I could say I didn't fancy him after all, and then …

Would it work? Would she fall for him?

'Don't tell Mum,' I said.

Mina pushed me away from her and laughed. 'Of course not, what do you take me for?'

The next day, when I told Serina, she clapped her hands.

'That's BRILLIANT, Laila! I knew you'd think of something. This way,

Mina won't be grumpy. She won't feel she's on show.'

'Do you think it will work?' I said, frowning.

'It's sure to,' said Serina. 'You wait! As soon as they see each other it'll be like – WOW! Instant attraction. They're both so good-looking, they're sure to fall for each other.'

'Umm,' I said.

I wasn't so sure.

'You and your mum will be there, won't you, Serina? Promise?'

'Of COURSE I will,' said Serina. 'Stop worrying. It will be fine. '

But I couldn't help worrying.

On Saturday morning, I was feeling
sick. I couldn't eat my breakfast.

Mum said, 'What's the matter,
Laila? Are you ill?'

I shook my head. 'Just not hungry.'

I looked across at Mina. She winked at me and smiled.

Mum was surprised when we said we wanted to go shopping with her – but she was pleased, too.

'Both my girls with me. That's lovely.'

When we reached the supermarket car park, I saw Serina and her mum getting out of their car. I waved at them and they came over.

Mum didn't know Serina's mum very well.

The two mums smiled at each other and started chatting. Mina, Serina and I moved away.

Mina whispered to me. 'It will be good if they get to know each other better. If Mum likes Karmal's family, it will be easier for you.'

Serina overheard Mina talking. She put her hand to her mouth to stop herself laughing, and I gave her a death stare.

She turned away, but I could see she was still giggling.

'Stop it,' I hissed.

The mums were still chatting as we went into the supermarket.

So far so good!

Mina grabbed a trolley and Serina and I walked either side of her.

We walked up and down the aisles, looking for the gorgeous Karmal.

'Where is this boy?' asked Mina.

'Er … I haven't seen him yet,' I said.

'Nor have I,' said Serina quickly.

36

'Well,' said Mina, starting to put stuff in her trolley. 'I'm going to do a bit of shopping. Let me know when you find him.'

Mina walked off and I nudged Serina in the ribs.

'He'd better be here!' I whispered.

Serina and I walked slowly round and round the supermarket. People were staring at us and I felt really stupid.

Round and round we went, up and

down every aisle, but there was no sign of the gorgeous Karmal.

Serina frowned. 'I'm sure he said he worked here on Saturday mornings,' she said.

Then suddenly she grabbed my arm and pointed. 'He's there! Look. Coming through the back doors!'

'Wow!' I whispered.

Karmal was coming out from the store room at the back, pushing a trolley loaded up with tins, packets and boxes.

He stopped for a moment and ran his hand through his hair.

'See? What did I tell you?' whispered Serina. 'Isn't he drop-dead gorgeous?'

I swallowed.

I was finding it difficult to speak and I couldn't take my eyes off him.

I nodded.

'Stop staring at him, Laila. Let's go and say hello.'

I tried to think straight.

'I must find Mina,' I said.

'In a minute,' said Serina. 'Let's say hello first.'

Serina took my arm and we walked over to Karmal. He was refilling the shelves from the stuff in his trolley.

'Hi Karmal,' said Serina.

'Hi cousin,' said Karmal, but he didn't stop what he was doing.

'This is my friend Laila,' said Serina.

Karmal turned round and looked at me. Then he smiled.

'Hi Laila,' he said, his eyes meeting mine. 'Good to meet you.'

'You too,' I stammered.

We wandered around near Karmal. I pretended to be interested in some tins of beans and Serina picked up a bag of potatoes and put it down again.

There was no sign of Mina.

I couldn't see her anywhere.

Suddenly we heard Mum's voice. She and Serina's mum were walking towards us.

'Quick,' said Serina. 'They'll be cross if they see us talking to Karmal.'

We ran towards them.

'Oh there you are,' said Mum. 'We've been looking for you.'

I turned and looked over my shoulder. Karmal had finished stacking the shelves and was heading back into the store room.

'I thought you said you wanted to do some shopping, Serina,' said her mum.

'Yes, we do,' said Serina quickly. 'We're just off to get a basket.'

She grabbed my hand and we headed towards the checkout to pick up a basket.

We set off again, looking for Mina.

'Mum will finish her shopping soon,'
I said. 'Then I'll have to go home. We
must get Mina and Karmal together.'

Then, at last, I spotted Mina. She
was trying out different shades of
lipsticks on the back of her hand.

'Mina,' I said. 'Come quickly! We've
found Karmal.'

'Umm,' she said. 'I saw you talking
to him. I don't think you need me. You
were doing fine on your own.'

I pulled at her arm. 'No I wasn't,'

I said. 'I couldn't think of anything to say to him. Please, Mina! Please come. I won't feel so shy if you're with me.'

Mina sighed and dropped a lipstick into her trolley.

'Oh, all right,' she said. 'Take me to lover boy.'

As we hurried away, Serina whispered, 'You're a good actress, Laila. I think Mina really believes you fancy Karmal.'

I didn't answer.

As we reached the door into the store room, Karmal came out with another loaded trolley.

'Hello again,' he said, when he saw us.

Then he walked on.

I couldn't believe it. He hardly glanced at Mina, but just pushed his trolley past her and began stacking the shelves.

Usually Mina makes boys go all soppy.

As soon as they see her they start to stutter and stammer and show off, but Karmal didn't even notice her.

Serina coughed. 'Karmal, this is Mina. She's Laila's sister.'

'Hi,' said Karmal, without turning round.

'Let the poor boy alone,' said Mina, laughing. 'Can't you see he's busy?'

Karmal looked at his watch. 'Yes,' he said. 'I finish work soon and I still have a lot to do.'

Mina dragged us away.

I tugged at her sleeve. 'What do you think, Mina?' I whispered. 'Isn't he gorgeous?'

'Yes, he's certainly good-looking. I can see why you fancy him, but you need to get to know him, Laila. Find out what he's like. Looks aren't everything.'

Serina winked at me, but I frowned. This wasn't going very well.

I wanted Mina to fancy him. I wanted Mina to get to know him.

Didn't I?

Mum was calling us over to the checkout:

'Come on girls. We need to go home now.'

I looked at Serina. 'What shall we do?' I whispered.

Serina shrugged. 'We can't do any more. We've introduced them.'

'But it hasn't worked. I was sure there'd be an instant spark. I was sure they'd fall for each other – just like that.'

'Maybe they did,' said Serina. 'It's hard to tell.'

I sighed.

'No,' I said. 'I don't think they did.'

I said goodbye to Serina and then I followed Mum and Mina out to the car park.

We were just putting the shopping into the car when I spotted Karmal coming out of the back of the supermarket. He was pushing a bike.

'I've forgotten something,' I yelled to Mum. 'I won't be long.'

I raced across the car park and round the edge of the supermarket building.

I didn't know what I was going to say to Karmal if I caught up with him.

But I had to have one more go at getting him and Mina together.

I was running so fast that I didn't realise that he had got on his bike and was coming round the corner of the building towards me.

He jammed on his bike brakes and I tried to dodge out of the way, but it was too late.

The next moment, Karmal had fallen

off his bike and I was lying bleeding on the ground beside him.

I wasn't badly hurt, but I was really upset and I was crying.

'I'm so sorry,' I sobbed. 'It all went wrong. I'm so sorry!'

Then I realised that Karmal was laughing.

He got up and put out his hand to me. He hauled me up.

I sniffed and wiped the blood off

my face with the back of my other
hand.

'I'm sorry,' I said again. 'I thought
you and Mina … I thought you would
fancy each other. Mum and Dad and the

aunties keep introducing her to boys she doesn't like and Serina said she had a cousin and … '

I stopped and put my hand over my mouth. What was I thinking, blurting all this out?

Karmal was still laughing. And he was still holding my hand.

'Laila,' he said. 'I promise you that your sister Mina doesn't need any help in finding a husband.'

'What do you mean?'

'Ask her about Asad.'

'What? Has she already met someone? How do you know?'

'Just ask her,' he said.

I looked at him properly then and our eyes met.

My tummy flipped over – but in a nice way.

He squeezed my hand. 'I hope you come shopping here every Saturday morning,' he said.

Then he released my hand and
mounted his bike.

I was still grinning when I got back
to the car.

Later that evening, I went into Mina's room. She was brushing her hair again.

I stood and watched her for a moment. Then I said, 'Tell me about Asad.'

The hairbrush fell from her hand and clattered to the ground.

She turned round and stared at me, her eyes huge.

'How do you know about Asad?'

'Karmal told me,' I said.

Mina was silent for a moment, then she said, 'I thought I'd seen Karmal somewhere before. I think he's at college with Asad.'

'So?' I said.

Mina sighed.

'Can you keep a big secret, Laila?'

I nodded and Mina went on. 'Do you promise not to tell Mum or Dad?'

'Of course I won't,' I said.

Mina moved over to her bed and sat down on it.

'I met Asad a year ago.'

'Was it love at first sight?'

'Yes,' said Mina, smiling. 'Right away we knew we were meant for each other.'

'Why can't you tell Mum and Dad about him?' I asked.

Mina fiddled with her hair. 'Because he's not a Pashtun boy,' she said quietly.

'Ah, I see.'

'So,' she went on, 'I want to wait until they think I'll never be married. Until they are desperate. Then I'll find a way of introducing them to him.'

'How?'

Mina smiled. 'I might need your help there,' she said. 'Maybe Mum could meet him in the supermarket!'

I laughed and sat down beside her. 'Tell me more about him.'

So she did.

'He sounds wonderful,' I said, when she'd finished.

'He is,' said Mina. 'And he'll be the perfect husband.'

MORE GREAT READS
IN THE PROMISES SERIES

Yasmin's Journey
by Miriam Halahmy

Fifteen-year-old Yasmin lives with her parents and younger brother Ali in a small town in Syria.

The country is at war and Yasmin is forced to leave Syria with Ali to find a new life for them both.

Travelling through the refugee camps of Turkey and Greece, Yasmin strikes up a friendship with sixteen-year-old Kamal. Can they all find peace and safety together?

Forevery
by Anne Rooney

In 1831 the Lightfoot family moved to a new house. On their first Sunday in church they hear the story of the long-dead knight Sir Edward d'Estur, who had gone off to fight in the Crusades. From that moment Lucy was captivated, visiting the church often. So begins a romantic ghost story, linking two distant pasts across five hundred years.